Pat Hutchins

The Silver Christmas Tree

THE BODLEY HEAD
LONDON

JP
435780

For Sam

Squirrel was busy decorating his tree for Christmas.
He hung garlands of holly and ivy around the branches,
bunches of bright red berries between the branches,
and pine cones on the tips of the branches.
And although it looked nice,
it didn't look quite nice enough.

So he hung strings of polished nuts on the tree,
tied bunches of mistletoe around the tree,
and stuck dried heads of wheat into the pine cones
on the tips of the branches.
And although the tree looked nicer,
it still didn't look nice enough.

Squirrel worked so hard, and so late,
that it became too dark to see the tree at all.

But at that very moment,
right on the very top branch of the tree,
a beautiful silver star appeared.
The tree looked wonderful!
Squirrel was delighted.
He would show his lovely
silver Christmas tree to his friends
on Christmas Eve, as a special present.

Squirrel slept happily that night and didn't wake up
until the sun was quite high in the sky.
Then he raced down the tree to admire his silver star.
But when he gazed up into the branches,
the lovely star had vanished!
And his beautiful silver tree wasn't silver any more.

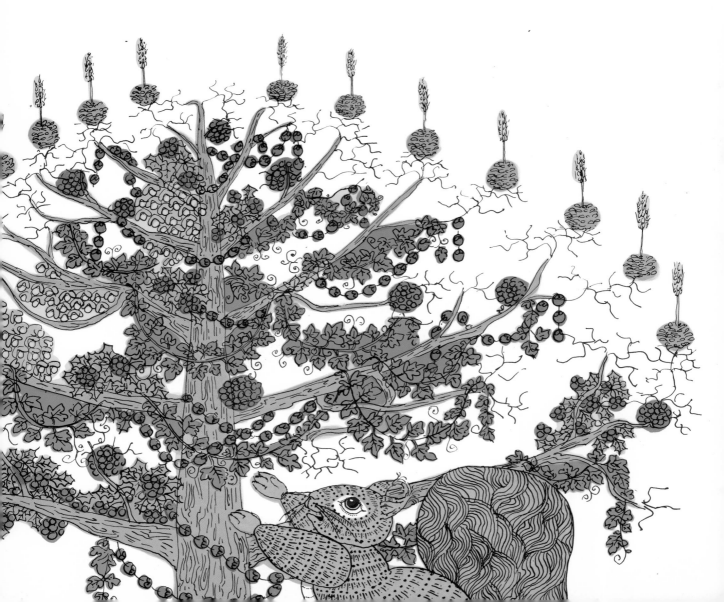

Squirrel searched in the tree,
around the tree,
and under the tree.
But he couldn't find the silver star.
So he went to ask his friend Duck
if he'd seen it.

His friend Duck was hiding a parcel in the rushes.
"Ah," thought Squirrel,
"my friend Duck has found my star for me."
"Duck," he said, "is that my star you've found
  hidden in the rushes?"

Duck smiled.

"Aha!" he said. "You will have to wait until Christmas Eve
  to find out what is hidden in those rushes!"

"So," thought Squirrel sadly as he walked away,

"Duck has my star."

On his way home he passed
his friend Mouse, who was putting
a parcel behind a stone wall.
"Ah!" thought Squirrel,
"I knew my good friend Duck
wouldn't take my star.
I see Mouse has found it for me!"

"Mouse," he said, "is that my star you've found
hidden behind that stone wall?"
"Aha!" Mouse smiled. "You must wait
until Christmas Eve to find out what is
hidden behind that stone wall!"
"So," thought Squirrel sadly as he walked away,
"Mouse has my star."

Then he passed his friend Fox, who was tucking
a parcel into his lair.
"Ah!" thought Squirrel. "I knew my good friend
Mouse wouldn't take my star.
I see Fox has found it for me!"

"Fox," he said, "is that my star you've tucked into your lair?"
"Aha!" Fox smiled. "You must wait until Christmas Eve
  to find out what is hidden in my lair!"
"So," thought Squirrel sadly as he walked away,
"Fox has my star."

But then Squirrel saw his friend Rabbit,
who was slipping a parcel down his burrow.
"Ah!" thought Squirrel. "I knew my good friend Fox
wouldn't take my star.
I see Rabbit has found it for me."

"Rabbit," he said, "is that my star
  you're slipping down your burrow?"
"Aha!" Rabbit smiled. "You will have to wait
  till Christmas Eve to find out
  what is hidden in my burrow!"

So Squirrel went home and waited.

The next day Rabbit, Fox, Mouse, and Duck arrived.
"Happy Christmas, Squirrel!" shouted Rabbit,
  handing Squirrel a parcel.
"This must be the star," thought Squirrel,
  but it felt too soft to be a star.

And it wasn't.

It was a soft fluffy blanket.

"Thank you, Rabbit," said Squirrel sadly. "It will keep me nice and warm through the winter. It's the nicest blanket I've ever had."

"Happy Christmas, Squirrel," said Fox,
handing Squirrel a parcel.
"Fox must have had the star after all,"
thought Squirrel, but it felt too long
to be a star.

And it wasn't.

It was a long silky duster.

"Thank you, Fox," said Squirrel sadly.

"It will do nicely for dusting my tree.

It's the nicest duster I've ever had."

"Happy Christmas, Squirrel," said Mouse,
  handing Squirrel a parcel.
"So," thought Squirrel, "it was little Mouse
  who had the star."
  But it felt too round to be a star.

And it wasn't.

It was a little round corn cake.

"Thank you, Mouse," said Squirrel sadly.

"It's my favourite kind of cake and
the nicest cake I've ever had."

And then Duck handed Squirrel a parcel.
"Ah!" thought Squirrel happily.
"This must be the star."
But it felt too square
to be a star.

And it wasn't the star either.

It was a square basket, woven from rushes.

"Thank you, Duck," said Squirrel sadly.

"It will be very handy for storing my nuts.

And it's the nicest basket I've ever seen."

Then Squirrel pointed to his tree.
"And there's my present to you," he said.
But it was nearly dark, and his friends
couldn't see anything.

But then all the animals stared in wonder,
for soft flakes of snow were falling from the sky,
and as they fell, the clouds parted.
Climbing up to the top branch of the tree was the silver star,
bigger, brighter, and more beautiful than ever.

The glow from the tree lit up Squirrel's face.
"Happy Christmas, everyone," he whispered.
"Happy Christmas!"
And all his friends thought it was the nicest present of all.